First published in Great Britain in 2007
by Zero To Ten Limited
2A Portman Mansions, Chiltern Street,
London W1U 6NR

This edition © 2007 Zero To Ten Limited
© Gallimard Jeunesse 2006

First published in France in 2006 as
Rita et Machin

British Library Cataloguing in Publication Data:
Arrou-Vignod, Jean-Philippe, 1958-
Rita and Whatsit
1. Rita (Fictitious character : Arrou-Vignod) - Juvenile
fiction 2. Whatsit (Fictitious character) - Juvenile
fiction 3. Children's stories
I. Title
843.9'14[J]

ISBN 9781840895100

Printed in China

JEAN-PHILIPPE ARROU-VIGNOD ✳ OLIVIER TALLEC

Rita and Whatsit

ZERO TO TEN

It's her birthday, but Rita is sulking.

She's not happy
about the presents.

There are too many.

Some are too big,

some are too small,

and some are just too
middle-sized!

Which one should she
open first?

Suddenly, the parcel in the corner
starts to wriggle about. Three little
jumps and it's off!

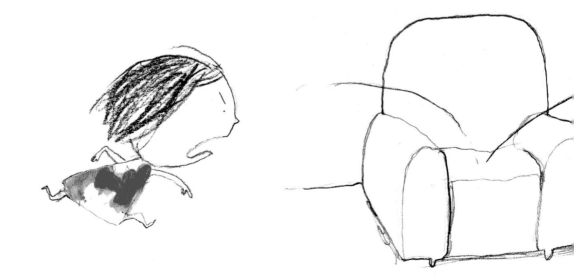

'Come back here, present,
or I'll tear you apart!'

A present that runs off –
that's a new one!
Whatever can it be?

A little scrap of a dog pokes out its nose. It glances sideways at Rita – and carries on doing its exercises.

'What?' cries Rita, 'I warn you, scrap-of-a-dog, if you are just another soft toy you'll go straight in the bin!'

The little dog doesn't reply, but his
heart thumps – ba-boom, ba-boom.

Rita brings him a big slice of birthday cake, some
milk, and handful of sweets.

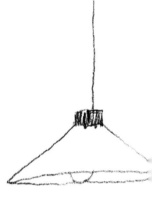

'Are you hungry, dog? Don't start burping, or I'll wrap you up in your box again.'

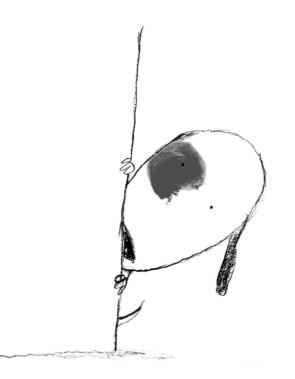

But the dog runs off.
'Come back here right now, dog!

If I'm going to keep you, you have to have a name. What about Wilhelm? Or Wellington?'
Rita scratches her head.

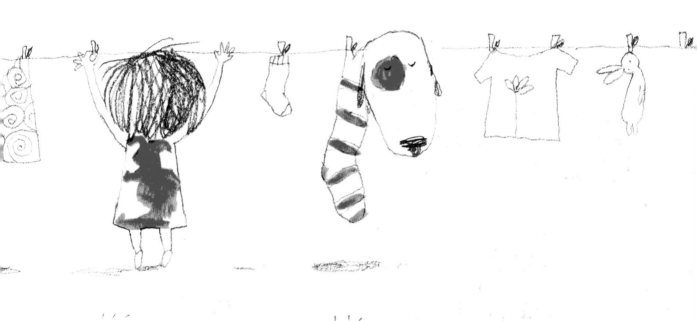

'No, not Wellington – you'd always want to give the orders. What about Sock? Come on, help me find a name, or don't you care?'

Rita can't get the dog to join in.
She shakes, scratches and tickles him,
but he just falls asleep.

'Don't start snoring! Not when we're just
getting to know one another! If you're not
careful I'll call you Floorcloth.
But then, who wants a dog called Floorcloth?'

'I've got it!' cries Rita. 'I could call you Whatsit!
That's a great name for a dog without a name.'

'Done!' says the dog. 'Give me five.'

Rita cannot believe her ears.
'Can you talk, Whatsit?'

'Only when I have to,' replies the dog.

'Well, Whatsit, I think we are going to be great
friends,' said Rita.
'Me too,' says Whatsit. 'But now I need
a nap. Have you got any pyjamas for me?'

Rita's birthday is nearly over. In her
bedroom all is quiet.

Is she still sulking? No, she's fast asleep, tired out after
opening all her new presents with her new friend.

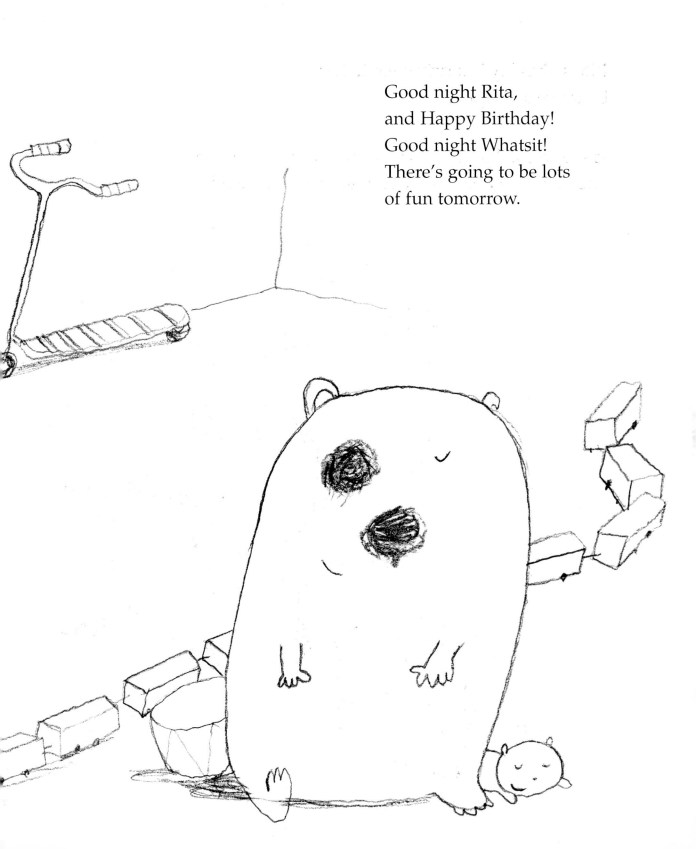

Good night Rita,
and Happy Birthday!
Good night Whatsit!
There's going to be lots
of fun tomorrow.